P9-EFI-217

Disney PRESS
Los Angeles • New York

All illustrations by the Disney Storybook Art Team
Published by Disney Press, an imprint of Disney Book Group.

For information address Disney Press, 1200 Grand Central Avenue, Glendale, California 91201.
This special edition was printed for Kohl's Department Stores, Inc.
(for distribution on behalf of Kohl's Cares, LLC, its wholly owned subsidiary),
by Disney Press, an imprint of Disney Book Group, Los Angeles/New York.

Kohl's
Style Number 9781368043106
Factory Number 131635
06/18-08/18

Printed in the United States of America

First Hardcover Edition, August 2018
1 3 5 7 9 10 8 6 4 2
FAC-131635-18222
ISBN 978-1-368-04310-6

CONTENTS

A DAY AT THE BEACH

"Come on, boys. Let's go!" Mickey called. He and Minnie had planned a big surprise for Mickey's nephews, Morty and Ferdie.

"Are we going to play ball?" Morty guessed.

"Or maybe fly a kite?" asked Ferdie.

"Even better! We're going to spend the whole day at the beach!" Mickey announced.

"Hooray!" the boys cheered. Pluto was so excited that he started chasing his tail.

There was a lot to do to get ready for a day at the beach. Minnie used her bows to make a new tail for the boys' kite while Mickey blew up the beach ball. Morty and Ferdie gathered the sunblock, the beach towels, and all their toys, of course.

"There's just one more thing we have to do before we leave," Minnie said. "Pack our picnic!"

Minnie and Mickey helped the boys make their favorite sandwiches. Then everyone worked together to fill the picnic basket with yummy things to eat.

"Whoops—we can't forget a treat for Pluto!" Minnie giggled as she added a bone to the picnic basket.

When they got to the beach, Morty and Ferdie helped Mickey and Minnie unload the car. Finally, everything was set up.

"Last one in the ocean is a rotten barnacle!" Mickey called.

Mickey and the boys splashed in the ocean. Pluto joined in the fun, too . . . until he got distracted by a crab!

Meanwhile, Minnie spread out the picnic blanket and opened the basket. “Lunch is ready!” she called to the boys.

Morty raced out of the water and grabbed his sandwich. The smell of cheese, lettuce, tomatoes, and pickles made his mouth water. He was about to take a big bite when suddenly—*whoosh*—his sandwich disappeared!

“Hey!” Ferdie yelled. “That seagull stole your sandwich!”

"My sandwich!" Morty howled.

"I'm sorry, Morty," Minnie replied. "Luckily, we have lots of other food to share."

But Morty just shook his head. "That was my favorite sandwich, though," he said sadly.

Ferdie tugged on Mickey's arm. "Come on, Uncle Mickey," he said. "Let's rescue Morty's sandwich."

"I guess it's worth a try," Mickey said. "Follow that gull!"

"Pluto and I will stay here and guard the rest of our picnic," Minnie said. "Good luck!"

The seagull swooped through the sky, casting a shadow over the sand. Mickey, Morty, and Ferdie charged after it. Near the water, Goofy was building a village of sandcastles.

"Hiya, Mickey!" Goofy called. "Where are you going in such a hurry?"

"We're on a sandwich rescue mission!" Mickey replied as he ran past his friend.

A little farther down the beach, Donald and Daisy were flying kites with Huey, Dewey, and Louie. In the sky, the seagull zigged and zagged through the kite strings. But down on the sand, it was a little harder for Mickey and his nephews to get past them.

"Be careful!" cried Daisy.

"Yeah—watch out for the strings!" Donald added.

"And the sand!" Huey yelled, shielding his eyes as Mickey and his nephews kicked up clouds of sand.

"Look, boys!" Mickey called. "The seagull is headed for the cliffs!"

The seagull glided effortlessly on the ocean breeze. Below, Mickey, Morty, and Ferdie made their way across the tide pools to reach the cliffs. The wet sand slowed them down, squishing and squelching under their feet. Mickey and his nephews tiptoed through the water, careful to avoid stepping on the starfish, clams, and sea anemones. They reached the cliffs just as the seagull disappeared over the rocky ledge.

Mickey, Morty, and Ferdie stared up at the cliff. It seemed very high.

"What do we do now, Uncle Mickey?" Ferdie asked.

"Well," Mickey said, "we can go back to Minnie and Pluto and enjoy the rest of our picnic . . . or we can climb the cliff and keep searching for that seagull."

"Let's climb!" Morty replied. By then he was so hungry he could practically taste his favorite sandwich. He couldn't wait to get it back.

Inch by inch, step by step, Mickey and his nephews scaled the rocky cliff. It was even harder than dodging the sandcastles, slipping through the kite strings, and crossing the tide pools!

Finally, they reached the top of the tallest ridge.

"Hold on a minute, boys," Mickey whispered. "Before we climb over the edge, we need a plan."

"I've already got one," Morty said. "As soon as I see that seagull, I'm going to swoop in and snatch my sandwich—just like it did to me!"

Morty hoisted himself up to the edge of the cliff . . . and froze. The seagull—and the sandwich—were just inches from Morty's face. But the seagull wasn't alone. It was perched on the side of a grassy nest next to three baby gulls! From the way the chicks were squawking, Morty could tell they were just as hungry as he was. Maybe even hungrier!

Morty watched for a moment as the seagull tossed bits of his sandwich to her babies. Then he began to climb back down the cliff to where Mickey and Ferdie were waiting. The seagull needed the sandwich more than he did.

Back on the beach, Morty told Minnie and Pluto all about the baby seagulls sharing his sandwich.

"What an adventure!" Minnie exclaimed. "But don't worry, Morty. We still have lots of food in our picnic basket. Here, I packed extra bread. And you can have the cheese from my sandwich."

"Take my pickle!" Mickey offered.

"And my tomato!" Ferdie added.

"Thanks, everybody!" Morty said. He grinned as he took a big bite of his brand-new sandwich. It tasted even better than it looked!

LOST AND FOUND

One spring morning, Mickey woke up and looked outside. It was a perfect day. The sky was blue, the air was fresh, and a gentle breeze blew through the trees. Mickey smiled to himself. A day like that meant only one thing: an adventure was in order!

There was just one problem. Mickey didn't know what he wanted to do!

Mickey sat down to think. What should he do with his day? Then he sat up straight. He could work in the garden! He could plant some more flowers and vegetables so that his garden would be complete. Then Mickey let out a sigh. That wouldn't work. He didn't have any seeds.

Mickey went back to thinking. Suddenly, he sat up straight again. He had it this time—the perfect idea! He could go to the farmers market and pick up something sweet for Minnie. Mickey looked down at his watch and sighed. It was too early. The farmers market wasn't open yet.

Just then, Mickey heard a noise in his front yard. Walking to the window, he saw his friend Goofy sitting on a bike.

"Hiya, Mickey!" Goofy called. "Want to go for a ride?"

"That's a great idea!" Mickey said happily. "I'd love to!"

Mickey laughed. He hadn't had to come up with an adventure—the adventure had come to him!

Mickey grabbed his own bike, and he and Goofy headed off down the road.

As they turned onto the bike path, Mickey looked around. Everywhere he looked, there were signs of spring. The friends passed by a field full of bright yellow flowers that filled the air with a wonderful smell.

"Look!" Mickey exclaimed as they rode farther down the road. "Up in that tree!" In the branches, a family of birds was making a nest. They chirped happily as they fluttered back and forth.

Mickey was so busy looking at the birds that he didn't notice a large branch on the path in front of him. As he rode over the branch, his tires began to wobble. Then his handlebars began to wobble. Soon he had lost control of his bike! Before he could even let out a shout, Mickey flew off the path and careened into the woods.

On the path, Goofy kept pedaling. He had no idea that Mickey was no longer with him.

Mickey bounced and bumped his way over rocks and sticks until, finally, he got control of his bike. He came to a stop, climbed off his bike, and took a look around.

He was in a part of the woods he had never been in before. Mickey shivered as he realized something: he was lost!

“I’d better figure out how to get back to the path,” Mickey said to himself. “I don’t want Goofy to worry about me.” Just then, Mickey heard a rustling behind him. “And I’m not so sure I want to be out here alone, either!”

Mickey jumped onto his bike and began to pedal back toward the path. Or at least, he *hoped* he was going toward the path. But the farther he pedaled, the wilder the woods around him grew.

At first, Mickey was nervous. Biking through the woods wasn't the same as biking on the path. But as he went, Mickey couldn't help noticing that it was beautiful in its own way.

"This isn't so bad," Mickey said. "It's actually kind of pretty. And the animals aren't all that scary." Mickey waved hello to a mother possum carrying her babies on her back. He spotted a hedgehog, some squirrels, even a fox. He waved hello to them, too.

The one thing Mickey didn't see was the path home.

As Mickey looked around the forest, he had a thought. The day was probably half over! He didn't want to get stuck in the woods after dark. Possums and hedgehogs were cute, but what kind of animals would he run into at night?

Mickey began to pedal faster.

And then he stopped short.

There, right in front of him, was a picture-perfect pond!

Mickey put his finger to his chin. He was thinking—but this time it wasn't about where to go for the day. He had just found the perfect place to go any day!

"This would be a great place for a picnic!" he shouted happily. "I can't wait to tell Goofy!"

He took one last look at the pond and turned around. He was more determined than ever to get back on the path and find Goofy.

Mickey pedaled and pedaled. Soon the forest grew thinner. Then, almost as quickly as he had gone off the path, he found himself back on it.

Suddenly, Goofy rounded the corner. "Mickey!" he shouted, startled to see his friend ahead of him. "Weren't you behind me?"

Mickey laughed. Goofy hadn't even known he was gone. "I got lost!" he said. "I've been riding through the woods this whole time! Wait till you hear what I found!"

As they rode back home, Mickey told his friend all about the pond. “There’s a rock where we can lay out our picnic,” he said. “And there’s a perfect branch for a rope swing.”

Together, Mickey and Goofy went to the farmers market. They grabbed sandwiches and fruit and gathered it together in a picnic basket. They bought a big blanket to sit on. Then Mickey stopped by the flower shop and got some flowers to take with him.

The only thing left to do was get their friends. Mickey and Goofy gathered everyone together and led them to the path. "Come on," Mickey said. "I have a surprise for you!"

He led them through the woods—which didn't seem nearly as scary with his friends by his side—and straight to the pond.

"It turns out I needed to get lost to find this place!" Mickey said. "But I'm sure glad I did."

The others agreed. Mickey had found them their new favorite swimming spot!

THE MISSING DAFFODILS

One day, Daisy Duck went to her friend Minnie's house to help in the garden. But when the two got outside, they found a big surprise. Minnie's daffodils were gone!

"This is terrible," Daisy said. "It must be a flower prowler!"

They found a few strands of fuzzy white hair on a bush near the daffodil patch.

"Maybe the flower prowler left it," Minnie said.

"Maybe," Daisy said. "Or it could be some of Figaro's hair."

A moment later, Minnie's doorbell rang. Mickey Mouse was standing on the porch with a big bunch of daffodils! Tied around them was a fluffy white ribbon.

"Oh, Mickey," Minnie cried. "How could you? You cut down my daffodils!"

Mickey looked confused. "What do you mean, Minnie?" he asked. "I bought these at the flower shop because I know you love daffodils!"

"Really?" Minnie said, putting the flowers in a vase. She was glad that Mickey wasn't the flower prowler.

Minnie, Daisy, and Mickey decided to look around town for the flower prowler. They headed to the park and found Goofy. He was wearing a big daffodil on his vest. And he was playing with a yo-yo that had a fuzzy white string!

"Hiya, Minnie," Goofy called. "Do you like my flower? Mr. Power is having a sale on daffodils today!"

"Hmmm . . ." said Minnie. "That's quite a coincidence."

"Maybe we'd better check out the flower shop," Daisy said.

The four friends went to Power's Flowers and peeked through the window.

"That's Mr. Power," Mickey said.

Minnie saw that the shopkeeper had a sharp pair of scissors and a fuzzy white mustache. And his shop was full of daffodils!

"He did it!" she cried. "I know it!"

POWER'S FLOWERS
DAFFODIL SALE

Minnie and her friends burst into the shop. “Where did you get these daffodils?” Minnie asked.

“From a farmer named Mrs. Pote,” Mr. Power answered. “She delivers daffodils here every day. But today she brought dozens of extras!”

Mr. Power pointed the way to Mrs. Pote’s farm. “You can’t miss her,” he said. “She has fuzzy white hair.”

Mrs. Pote's farm was called Pote's Goats.

"Yes, I delivered extra daffodils today," Mrs. Pote told Minnie. "My favorite goat, Flower, usually eats a lot of them as soon as they bloom. But she must not have been very hungry today."

That gave Minnie an idea. "May I see Flower?" she asked.

"Of course, dear," Mrs. Pote said. She led the friends to a pen. But there was no goat inside!

"Oh, my!" Mrs. Pote cried. "She must have escaped! Wherever could she have gone?"

"Look! There's a hole in the fence," Mickey said, pointing.

"Now what do we do?" Daisy exclaimed. "Not only are Minnie's daffodils gone, but so is Mrs. Pote's goat!"

"Hmmm . . ." said Minnie, deep in thought. "Maybe these two mysteries are connected!"

“What do you mean, Minnie?” Daisy asked.

“I have an idea who the flower prowler might be,” Minnie explained. “It’s someone who really likes daffodils. Someone who likes them even more than we do!”

Daisy held up the fuzzy strands of hair. "Don't forget this," she reminded Minnie. "Isn't it still a clue?"

"It sure is," Minnie agreed. "And so is this!" She pointed toward a trail of footprints. "Follow me!"

Minnie and the others followed the footprints straight to Daisy's yard. There was Flower, happily munching away on Daisy's flowers.

"See?" Minnie said. "I knew it! There's our flower prowler. Now if we could only train her to like weeds instead!"

GOOFY AT THE RANCH

Minnie Mouse was excited. She, Mickey, and Goofy were going to the Lucky Star Dude Ranch. But Mickey was still packing.

"Come on, Mickey!" Minnie shouted to Mickey. "I want to learn how to ride a horse!"

"Be right there, Minnie," Mickey shouted downstairs as he put the last of his clothing in his suitcase.

Goofy was excited to ride a horse, too. The minute they reached the ranch, he hopped on the first horse he saw. But he jumped on it backward!

"Uh-oh!" Goofy cried as the horse bucked. "Now what do I do?"

Luckily, Minnie had brought a bunch of carrots with her to feed the horses. She held one out to the horse, and it happily trotted over to eat it.

"Whew! That was close!" Goofy gasped. "Thank goodness you were here, Minnie!"

Minnie and her friends went inside to change into their riding clothes. When they came back out, the owner of the ranch was waiting for them. "Howdy, cowgirl," he said to Minnie. "I'm Cowboy Bob. How 'bout we get you up on that horse?"

Cowboy Bob helped Minnie onto a horse. In no time she was riding like a pro.

“This isn’t so hard,” said Goofy a little while later as he trotted by on a horse. “Hey, Cowboy Bob, can you teach me how to use a lasso?”

“You betcha, Goofy,” Cowboy Bob said. “Just swing the rope over your head like this. Then aim and let go!”

Goofy hopped off his horse and tried to follow Cowboy Bob's example. "I'm going to lasso that hitching post," he said.

Goofy whirled the lasso and let go. But instead of catching the post, he caught his foot!

"Whoops!" Goofy cried.

“Looks like you could use some more practice, Goofy,” Mickey said.

Minnie giggled. “Mickey and I are going to go for a ride,” she said. “We’ll see you when you get yourself untangled, Goofy.”

For three days, Minnie, Mickey, and Goofy learned how to be cowboys. On their last morning at the ranch, they planned to watch the rodeo.

Cowboys from all over gathered to watch the show. Minnie and Goofy sat in the stands. “I wonder where Mickey is,” said Minnie, watching. “He really wanted to see this!”

But Mickey was still asleep! He had forgotten to set his alarm clock.

As the noisy crowd passed by his window, it woke him up. Mickey looked at the time. He had to hurry or he would miss all the fun!

Mickey quickly got dressed and dashed out the door. He raced across a field, jumped over a fence . . . and landed right on a bucking bronco in the middle of the rodeo!

Everyone cheered as Mickey held tightly to the reins.

"Hey! This is sort of fun!" he cried.

As Mickey waved his hat to the crowd, the announcer cried out, "Mickey Mouse has just broken the ranch record for the longest-ever bronco ride!"

Just then, the bronco bucked again and Mickey slid off.

"Oh, no!" Minnie shouted. "We have to help Mickey!"

"I'll lasso it for you, Mickey!" shouted Goofy. But instead of lassoing the bronco, he lassoed Mickey.

Meanwhile, Minnie hopped over the fence and led the bronco safely back to his stall.

Later that day, the crowd cheered as Cowboy Bob presented the rodeo ribbons.

Minnie won for taking good care of the horses. Mickey won for his bronco riding. And Goofy won for trying to lasso everything in sight!

Later that night, Minnie sat by the campfire with her friends.

"This has been so much fun," she said. "I can't believe we have to leave tomorrow!"

Just then, Minnie spotted an odd shape against the moon. "Hey, look! A coyote! Now I really feel like a cowgirl!"

"Want me to lasso him?" asked Goofy.

Minnie giggled. "Thanks, Goofy, but I think he's better off where he is!"

And with another giggle, she went back to enjoying the campfire.

THE TREE HOUSE

One sunny morning, Mickey had an idea. He was going to build a tree house! Mickey called all his friends and asked if they would like to help.

Soon Minnie, Donald, Daisy, and Goofy arrived in Mickey's yard.

“Building a tree house is a big job. Maybe we should split up the work,” Mickey said. “Why don’t you saw the boards, Goofy? Then Donald and I can hammer them together.”

“I have an idea,” Minnie said. She showed Mickey a special drawing she had made.

“Good thinking, Minnie!” Mickey replied. “That will be one of the most important jobs of all.”

Goofy dumped out his toolbox in a corner of the yard. The tools made a big *crash*—and a big mess! Goofy found what he was looking for and began sawing the boards.

After a few minutes, Minnie walked up to him. “Sorry to bother you, Goofy,” she began. “I was wondering if you would cut some boards for me, too.”

“Sure!” Goofy said with a grin. “Just tell me what you need.”

Goofy took a look at Minnie’s drawing. Then he cut some boards and helped her carry them across the yard.

Over by the big tree, Donald and Mickey worked together to make a rope ladder. When they were finished, Mickey attached the ladder to the thickest branch. He gave the ladder a strong tug. It didn't budge.

"That should do it," Mickey said. "Once we finish building, we can use this ladder to climb into the tree house."

Just then, Goofy brought them a stack of boards. "Here you go!" he said proudly. "I still have to saw the boards for the roof, but you can use these for the floor and the walls."

"Thanks, Goofy!" Mickey said.

Mickey and Donald climbed into the tree, pulling the boards behind them. The sound of their hammers echoed through the backyard as Mickey and Donald started building.

Across the yard, Minnie pulled her hammer out of her tool belt. As she picked up the first board, she realized that she had forgotten something very important.

Minnie hurried over to the big tree. "Do you have any extra nails?" she called up. "I left all of mine at home!"

"I have some," Donald said. He fished a box of nails out of his tool belt and gave them to Minnie.

On the way back to her project, Minnie stopped to see how Daisy was doing.

"Wow, Daisy," Minnie said. "You mixed up a *lot* of paint!"

Daisy giggled. "I might have mixed a little too much," she said. "Do you need any paint for your project?"

"Thanks, Daisy," Minnie said. "That would be great!"

Buzz-buzz-buzz went the saw.

Bang-bang-bang went the hammers.

Swish-swish-swish went the paintbrushes.

Mickey's backyard was a very busy place!

Later that day, Morty, Ferdie, and Pluto came home from the park. Morty and Ferdie couldn't believe their eyes. "Wow!" the boys cried.

"That's the best tree house ever!" added Ferdie. Then they scrambled up the rope ladder.

But Pluto stayed behind. He tilted his head and stared at the ladder. He couldn't climb it like the others.

Mickey understood right away. “Don’t worry, Pluto!” he called. “Come around to the other side of the tree.”

Pluto trotted around the tree and found something that made his tail wag: a set of stairs that were just his size!

“Minnie made them for you,” Mickey explained. “Now come on up and join the fun!”

Pluto ran up the stairs. It really was the best tree house ever!